ROTTEN RALPH

Feels Rotten

Written by **Jack Gantos**

Illustrated by **Nicole Rubel**

Farrar Straus Giroux

New York

For Anne and Mabel —J.G.

For my family —N.R.

Text copyright © 2004 by Jack Gantos
Illustrations copyright © 2004 by Nicole Rubel
All rights reserved
Color separations by Hong Kong Scanner Arts
Printed in China by South China Printing Co. Ltd.,
Dongguan City, Guangdong Province
Designed by Nancy Goldenberg
First edition, 2004
5   7   9   10   8   6   4

www.fsgkidsbooks.com

Library of Congress Cataloging-in-Publication Data
Gantos, Jack.
    Rotten Ralph feels rotten / written by Jack Gantos ; illustrated by Nicole
Rubel.— 1st ed.
        p.   cm.
    Summary: Rotten Ralph comes to appreciate Sarah's healthy cat food after
he gets sick from eating out of trash cans.
    ISBN: 978-0-374-36357-4
    [1. Cats—Fiction.   2. Food habits—Fiction.]   I. Rubel, Nicole, ill.   II. Title.

PZ7.G15334Rof 2004
[E]—dc22
                                                                        2003049252

The character of Rotten Ralph was originally created by
Jack Gantos and Nicole Rubel.

Contents

Trash-Can Gourmet

At dinnertime, Sarah served Rotten Ralph a home-cooked meal. "I want you to finish everything on your plate," she said.

Rotten Ralph turned up his nose. His whiskers drooped. All these fruits and vegetables will finish me off, he said to himself.

"Just take one little bite," Sarah said, "or I'll have to give you a spoonful of cod liver oil."

Rotten Ralph sniffed his food. His eyes crossed. He slid off his chair and hid under the table.

"Have you been sneaking cat treats into your room?" Sarah asked.

Ralph shook his head. He knew the best treats were not hidden in his room.

"Well, no dessert for you," said Sarah. "And don't even think about raiding the refrigerator."

Ralph didn't. He knew there was nothing good in there anyway.

Sarah gave him a kiss good-night.
Ralph waited until she was sound
asleep. Then he climbed out his
window and sneaked into the alley.

Who needs a refrigerator, he thought, when I have all these trash cans? He rubbed his paws together. I wonder what is on the menu today?

He lifted a lid and got busy. He started with a green chicken wing. Then he nibbled on some squishy squid. After that he licked a furry fish. For dessert he found a hunk of blue cheesecake. Then he washed it all down with a carton of chunky chocolate milk.

I'm stuffed, Ralph groaned. He
picked his teeth and burped so loudly,
the dogs began to howl. Calm down,
Ralph thought. I'm born to eat trash.

He quietly climbed back through his window. He flopped down onto his soft bed. Nothing like going to sleep on a full belly, he said to himself. Sweet dreams to me.

A Bellyful of Trouble

That night, Ralph had a nightmare. He dreamed little rats with spears were jumping up and down on his belly.

In the morning, he opened his eyes and Sarah was poking him awake. "Ralph," she cried, "you were moaning in your sleep!"

She mopped his sweaty brow. "You look awful," she said. She gently rubbed his swollen belly. She checked his throat for a hair ball. When he meowed, his breath smelled worse than rotten.

Sarah saw the open window and a
fish head on Ralph's pillow. She was
suspicious. "Have you been eating out
of the trash cans again?" she asked.

Rotten Ralph nodded. He felt so sick,
he knew he had to tell the truth.

"Maybe you need a big healthy breakfast," Sarah said.

Don't talk about *food*, Ralph thought. He stuck his head out the window for some fresh air.

"I better get you to the vet," Sarah decided. "You might have eaten something too rotten—even for you."

Ralph remembered eating the green chicken, the squishy squid, the furry fish, the blue cheesecake, and the chunky chocolate milk. Suddenly, his stomach felt bad all over.

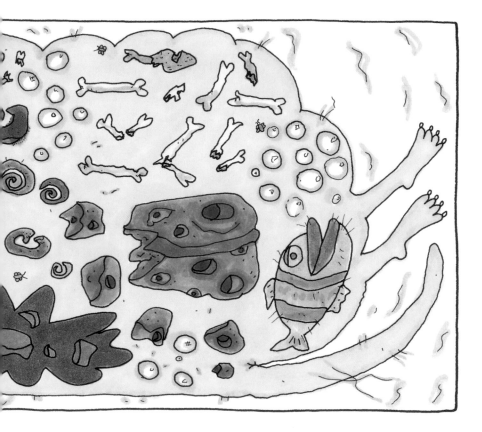

It rumbled and roared. Ralph
meowed miserably. Sarah ran and got
a bucket, just in case.

Hurry up and get me to the vet,
Ralph pleaded. I think I'm dying.

Sarah made a little pillow bed for
him in her red wagon. She got him
comfortable.

Quickly, she pulled him down the street toward the vet's office. All the way there, Ralph clutched his little spit-up bucket.

Tummy Toss

In the waiting room, Sarah propped
Ralph up in a chair. He was so weak,
he didn't even play in the fish tank. He
didn't hiss at the dogs, or tie the snake
in a knot.

"When it's our turn," Sarah said to
him, "I want you to be good and do
everything the vet tells you to do."

The nurse called them in.

"What's the problem?" the vet asked.

"I'm worried," said Sarah. "Ralph's been eating out of the trash again."

"I'll give him some tests," said the vet.

But Ralph was not in the mood for tests.

The vet slipped a thermometer under
Ralph's tongue. He spit it out.

"Ralph," Sarah said, "the vet is only
trying to help."

Next, the vet checked Ralph's reflexes. He hit him on the knee with a little rubber hammer. Ralph kicked the vet off his stool.

"Behave," said Sarah, "or you'll just feel worse."

When the vet went to check his ears,
Ralph jammed his paws in them.

"Ralph," said Sarah, "you need to
settle down."

I can't hear you, Ralph said to
himself.

The vet tried to listen to Ralph's
heart with a stethoscope. But Ralph
just burped out loud.

"Ugh," said the vet.

"Now, that's *rotten*," said Sarah.

"I've got just the medicine he needs," said the vet. "Hold him down."

They did.

The medicine didn't take long to work. Ralph threw up the green chicken, the squishy squid, the furry fish, the blue cheesecake, and the chunky chocolate milk.

Soon, Ralph felt like his old self again.

I'm better, he thought, rubbing his

empty belly. No more tests for me!

He jumped up and started to have some fun.

But the vet wasn't through yet.

"He's acting strangely," the vet said. "We'll have to hold him overnight for observation."

The nurse carried him away.

Don't let them take me, Ralph cried.

But there was nothing that Sarah could do.

Homesick

Being away from Sarah was worse than being sick. There was no one to fix him a nice snack. There was no one to tuck him in with a good book. There was just him and a bunch of sick puppies.

When the lights were turned down,
Ralph knew what he had to do. He
knocked off his covers and climbed out
the window.

He walked through the alley. There were plenty of fresh pickings in the trash cans, but he didn't eat any. He took a deep breath and held his nose all the way home.

He sneaked back into the house. He knew what he wanted—something healthy.

When Sarah woke up, she heard a
noise in the kitchen.

"Ralph! I'm so glad they let you come home early," Sarah said.

Me too, thought Ralph.

Then Sarah gave him a hug. "No more trash for you, Ralph."

Nothing like home cooking, he said to himself, and curled up on Sarah's lap.